The Bootmaker and the Elves

by Susan Lowell

pictures by Tom Curry

Orchard Books

New York

Once upon a time, there was a cowboy bootmaker who was so poor that even his shadow had holes in it.

Trouble was, the boots he made were just plain ugly, and they pinched so hard that nary a cowboy would buy them.

"Honey," he said to his wife one day, "we're plumb broke."

It was true. The bootmaker's wife was as skinny as a snake on stilts, and the bootmaker's own boots were so frazzled that he couldn't strike a match without burning his feet.

But he still had enough leather to make one last pair of boots. He cut them out before he went to bed, planning to start sewing the next day.

Bright and early, he went to his workbench — and his jaw dropped clear down to his kneecaps.

"Well, I'll be hornswoggled!" he cried.

"Great day in the morning!" gasped his wife, peering over his shoulder.

There stood a finished pair of beautiful boots — tall, shiny, and black as midnight under a skillet. The tops were hand-tooled with stars and roses, and smack-dab on the tip of each pointed toe was stitched a lucky horseshoe.

"But where did they come from?" asked the bootmaker's wife.

Dazed, the bootmaker just shook his head. He studied one of the boots and saw that every stitch and curve was perfect. These boots were masterpieces!

"It must be magic!" whispered the bootmaker's wife.

At that very moment, a customer moseyed into the shop. He was a rich rancher all feathered out in fancy duds and looking for footwear to match.

"Try these on for size, friend!" said the bootmaker.

The black boots fitted as though they were custom-made. Pulling out a wad of money big enough to choke a cow, the rancher paid the bootmaker so well that he went right out and bought enough leather to make two pairs of boots.

Meanwhile the bootmaker's wife bought enough beef for a barbecue.

Again the bootmaker cut the leather in the evening, left it on his workbench, and went to bed. And all night long he dreamed strange dreams of boots.

Next morning, he and his wife peeked into the shop, and there stood not one but two pairs of brand-new boots.

"Why, they're as pretty as a little red heifer in a flower bed!" cried the bootmaker's wife, all goggle-eyed with surprise. "More magic!"

Just then a customer banged open the door. He was a rootin' tootin' cowboy from the back of beyond.

This old cowpoke leaned his elbow on the counter and said, "I'm wild and woolly and full of fleas, and never been curried below the knees. I need boots!"

"Mister," said the bootmaker, "I have *just* the ones for you."

He lifted a pair off the workbench. They were high-heeled, knee-high, needle-nosed working boots made out of hairy spotted calf hide.

"Yippee! Yeow!" cried the cowboy, when he found they were a perfect fit. "I'm a wolf and it's my night to howl! Let 'er buck!"

The buckaroo went swaggering down the street, and soon afterward a new customer arrived. She was the best horse trainer in the whole territory.

"I can teach a wild mustang to turn on a biscuit and never break the crust," she said. "But my boots are worn to a shred."

"Ma'am," answered the bootmaker, "I have just the ones for you."

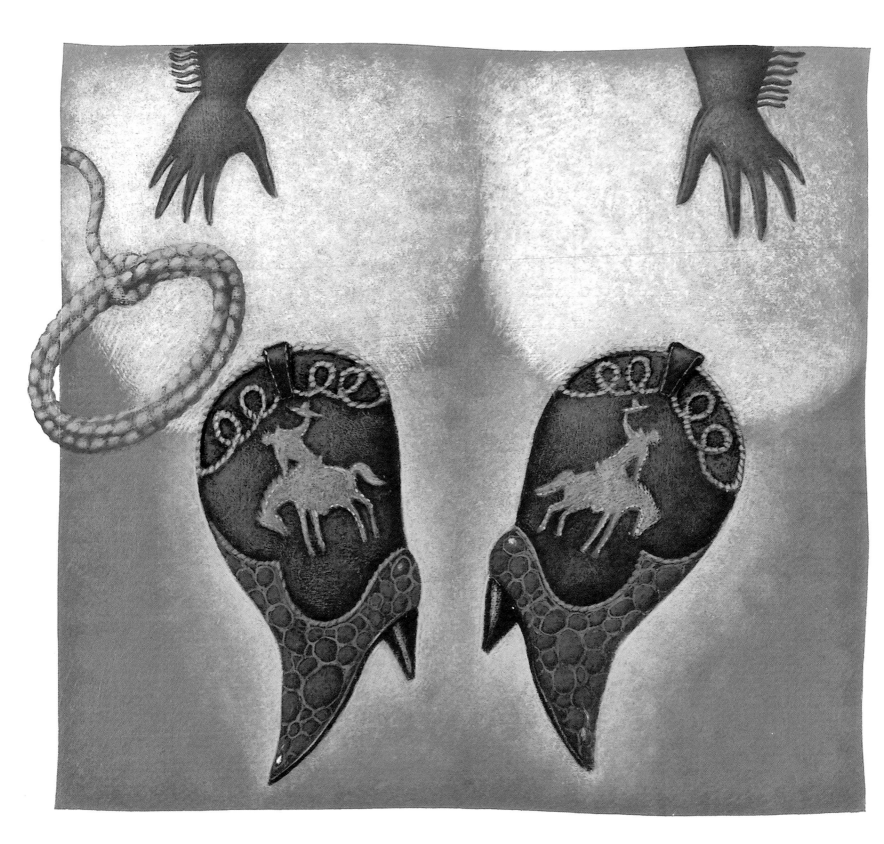

She put them on her feet and smiled. "Dee-licious!" she said.

Her new boots had chocolate cow-leather tops inlaid with bucking broncos, and the toes were made of lizard skin that glittered like a fresh-baked pecan pie.

The cowboy and the horse trainer paid the bootmaker enough to buy the leather to make four pairs of boots.

"This time," advised his wife, "get lots of colored leather too!"

And so he did. Once again, he cut the leather in the evening and went to bed, and once again boots went stamping, jumping, dancing through his dreams. In the morning the bootmaker rushed to his workbench.

Sure as shootin' the new leather was transformed into *four* pairs of cowboy boots.

The first pair were two giant boots with silver longhorn cattle on the front and golden oil derricks on the back, lone stars on the toes, and yellow roses in between. The bootmaker sold them to a big bowlegged man from Texas.

Clump! Clump! Out stomped the Texan, and in sashayed a rodeo queen, all ruffles and curls.

The bootmaker helped her into a pair of boots made of creamy glove leather, inlaid with lavender butterflies and pale pink hearts, and stitched in curlicues from top to bottom with sparkling thread. Those boots were so fine you could see the wrinkles in her socks!

"Mighty nice!" purred the rodeo queen.

The last two pairs were peewee boots, chile-pepper red and sky blue, decorated with suns and moons and rattlesnakes and cactus. The bootmaker sold those boots to a little cowboy and a little cowgirl.

"Ya-hoo!" they shouted, and skipped away.

And so it went. Every night the bootmaker left the leather, and every morning the magical boots appeared, and the bootmaker and his wife were in hog heaven. But they were also mighty curious.

"Honey," said the bootmaker to his wife one day, "why don't we hole up somewhere tonight, and find out who's helping us?"

His wife agreed, and so they lit a candle, hid in the closet, and kept their eyes peeled — till right at the stroke of midnight two cute little critters came tippytoeing into the room.

"Pack rats!" whispered the bootmaker. "Dad-ratted varmints!"

"Shh!" hissed his wife. "Those are *elves*!"

Hopping onto the workbench, the elves began to sew and hammer faster than greased lightning. The bootmaker rubbed his eyes in disbelief.

"Watch how they do it!" breathed his wife.

Scraps of crocodile, ostrich, buffalo, and buckskin flew through the air in all the colors of the rainbow. Fancy shapes and stitches flowered upon the leather. Bang! On went the high heels. Swish-swish-swish, and the boots were polished and set in a row, and lickety-split the elves were gone.

The next morning the bootmaker's wife said, "Those two little half-pints are making us rich, but they're running around in the cold without enough clothes to dust a fiddle."

"They sure look puny," the bootmaker agreed.

"I know what!" said his wife. "I'll make them each a brand-spanking-new outfit. You can make two pairs of itty-bitty boots!"

But before he set to work, the bootmaker sat still as a stone for a long time, thinking. Magical new ideas tickled his brain.

He daydreamed about boots . . . golden boots that sparkled with diamonds, rubies, and emeralds . . . feather-light boots that flew on soft silvery wings . . . and scaly brown rattlesnake boots that hissed and bit snakes back!

"Doggone it!" he said at last. "I'll put some fancy in *my* boots too!"

And he created four boots no bigger than a cowboy's thumb. They were as velvety as pea pods, greener than a hundred-dollar bill, and embroidered all over with a field of lucky clovers.

"Why, they're the best boots I ever saw!" cried his wife.

That evening, instead of leaving leather on the workbench, the bootmaker and his wife laid out two small sets of blue jeans, Western shirts, cowboy hats, socks, and marvelous miniature money-colored boots—and then they watched and waited.

Sure enough, right on the stroke of midnight the elves scurried into the room. When they discovered their presents, they were just as pleased as a little dog with two tails.

Everything was a perfect fit! Then their tiny toes began to tap, and the elves began to dance and sing:

"Whoopee-ki-yi-yay,
Now it's time to play!"

They did the polka down the workbench, do-si-doed amongst the chairs, and two-stepped round and round the bootmaker's shop, singing:

"Yo-de-lay-eee-ooo,
Happy trails to you!"

Then those two little elves scooted their boots right out the door, and nobody ever saw hide nor hair of them again.

But thanks to the elves, the bootmaker and his wife stayed fat and sassy ever after. And the boots that he made from leather and dreams were the best in the whole wide West.

To my mother and father, with love —S.L.

In memory of Max —T.C.

Text copyright © 1997 by Susan Lowell

Illustrations copyright © 1997 by Tom Curry

First Orchard Paperbacks edition 1999

Orchard Books, A Grolier Company

95 Madison Avenue, New York, NY 10016

Manufactured in the United States of America

Printed and bound by Phoenix Color Corp.

Book design by Chris Hammill Paul

Hardcover 10 9 8 7 6 5 4 3

Paperback 10 9 8 7 6 5 4 3 2

The text of this book is set in 24 point Golden Type-Original. The illustrations are rendered in acrylic drybrush technique on hardboard.

Library of Congress Cataloging-in-Publication Data

Lowell, Susan, date.

The bootmaker and the elves / by Susan Lowell; pictures by Tom Curry.

p.   cm.

Summary: A retelling, set in the Old West, of the traditional story about two elves who help a poor shoemaker, or in this case a bootmaker, and his wife.

ISBN 0-531-30044-7 (tr.) ISBN 0-531-33044-3 (lib. bdg.) ISBN 0-531-07138-3 (pbk.)

[1. Fairy tales. 2. Folklore—Germany.] I. Curry, Tom, ill. II. Wichtelmänner. English. III. Title.

PZ8.L9485Bo   1997   398.2—dc21   96-53303